ALL KINDS OF
TRUCKS

BY EDITH T. KUNHARDT
ILLUSTRATED BY ART SEIDEN

A GOLDEN BOOK · NEW YORK

WESTERN PUBLISHING COMPANY, INC., RACINE, WISCONSIN 53404

Copyright © 1984 by Western Publishing Company, Inc. Illustrations copyright © 1984 by Art Seiden. All
rights reserved. Printed in the U.S.A. No part of this book may be reproduced or copied in any form
without written permission from the publisher. GOLDEN®, GOLDEN® & DESIGN, and A GOLDEN
BOOK® are trademarks of Western Publishing Company, Inc. Library of Congress Catalog Card Number:
83-82601   ISBN 0-307-10406-0/ISBN 0-307-60403-9 (lib. bdg.)
A B C D E F G H I J

It is early morning. The sky is getting light. The milk truck is here. It brings fresh milk and eggs and butter for breakfast.

Every day the bakery truck delivers fresh bread
and rolls and cakes and pies to restaurants and stores.
The inside of the truck smells like warm bread.

Garbage and trash get thrown into the back of the garbage truck. The truck works hard to push its metal squeezer. The squeezer crushes boxes and cartons so that more garbage can fit in.

The automobile carrier hauls new cars from the automobile factory. It takes them to places where they will be sold. The cars look funny riding along with no drivers.

The gasoline truck brings gasoline to fill up the big tank under the gas station. Then the pump pumps the gas out of the tank and into the car

The postal truck takes the mail from mailboxes
to the post office. From there the letters are sent
all over the world.

Beeeeeeeep! The fire truck's air horn makes a low noise. *Whee! Whee!* shrieks its siren. The buildings are burning. Fire fighters climb the truck's ladder and help people climb down.

The dump truck is ready to dump a load of rocks. The body of the truck tilts up. *Rumble, rumble, rumble.* All the rocks slide down. They thump out onto the ground.

The cement mixer's tank turns around and
around. The cement inside the tank will get hard
if it stops moving.

It is time to make a new sidewalk. Down the
slide comes the cement. The workers spread it
out fast.

The tow truck has come to get a broken car.
The winch pulls the front of the car up in the air.
Now the truck will tow the car to the garage.

The farmer loads his pickup truck. He hopes
his giant pumpkin will win a prize at the fair.

Ding! Ding! The ice cream truck's bell is ringing. Ice cream cups, cones, and ices are for sale. When the freezer is opened, frosty air comes out.

Five horses go up the ramp of the horse van. Inside the van, they walk backward into their stalls. They are traveling to a horse show out of town. If they get hungry on the way, they can eat hay out of nets hanging from the ceiling.